# SUPER SAM

Written by Kaitlin Broadfoot
Illustrated by Kimberley Scott

Collins

Sam was a dog.
He slept in his basket all day,
dreaming of bones.
But he had a secret.

z z z z z z z

When his owners left, he became
Super Sam!
He put on his little red cape and
little red socks, and flew into the air,
searching for someone to rescue.

He was flying over the park one morning when he saw a puppy in need!

The puppy was scared.
It was clinging on to a branch
in the middle of the lake.

"Don't worry!" cried Super Sam.
"I'll save you!"
He zoomed down from the sky and picked up the puppy.

“Thank you, Super Sam.”
said the puppy.

Super Sam flew over the rooftops and through the window of his house.

He just had time to hang up his
little red cape and little red socks
before his owners arrived.

"Shame Sam can't be like this dog," said Sam's owner the next day, holding up the newspaper. On the front cover, it said: Super Dog Saves Puppy!

Sam rolled his eyes. If only they knew it was him!

# Super Dog

# Saves Puppy!

The puppy thanks Super Dog for saving him.

Super Dog flies home.

Super Dog saved the day again last night. He saved a puppy from falling in the lake. The puppy is now back with its owners, who would like to thank Super Dog!

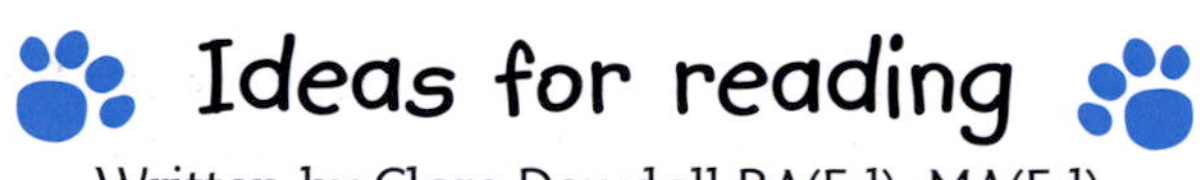


Written by Clare Dowdall BA(Ed), MA(Ed)
*Lecturer and Primary Literacy Consultant*

**Learning objectives:** identify the main events and characters in stories; make predictions showing an understanding of ideas, events and characters; retell stories ordering events using story language; explore familiar themes and characters through improvisation and role play

**Curriculum links:** Citizenship: Animals and us

**High frequency words:** was, a, dog, he, in, his, all, day, of, but, had, when, his, put, on, little, red, and, into, the, for, to, over, one, saw, it, don't, you, down, from, over, house, just, time, up, can't, be, like, this, next, on, said, they, him, home, again, last, night, from, now, back, with, who, would

**Interest words:** super, secret, owners, cape, rescue, zoomed, rooftops, shame, newspaper

**Resources:** pens, pencils

**Word count:** 170

## Getting started

- Ask children to name any superheroes that they know. As a group, discuss what superheroes do.
- Ask children to read the title and blurb aloud. Look at the front cover and discuss what Super Sam's secret is. Ask children to suggest what he might do when he is Super Sam.
- Focus on the blurb. Ask children to choose a tricky word and model how they read it, e.g. using familiar word endings and prefixes to read *own-ers; be-came.*

## Reading and responding

- Read pp2–3 aloud with the children. Look at the picture and ask children to find clues that Sam is a Super Dog, e.g. red cape and socks hanging up.
- Ask children to read pp4–5 aloud. Pause and ask children to predict who Sam might rescue.